WHAT WAS THAT!

by Geda Bradley Mathews   pictures by Normand Chartier

Golden Press • New York
Western Publishing Company, Inc.
Racine, Wisconsin

One cold winter night Baby Bear snuggled
down under the bed covers and shut his
eyes to go to sleep.

Then right in his room he heard an eek
and a creak and a squeak.

Baby Bear sat straight up in his bed.

"What was that?" he called out in the darkness. Then he skedaddled out of bed...

...down the hall, and *swoosh!* into bed with his big brother.

"I heard an eek right in my room," said Baby Bear from deep down under the covers, "and a creak and a squeak."

"Why, there's nothing to be frightened of," said the big brother bear. "Those noises were some little mice in their little mouse house getting ready for bed.

"That eek was a baby mouse. He said, 'Eek!' when he slid his bare feet down between the cold, cold sheets. The creak was the sound of the bed springs creaking when he turned over on his side to go to sleep. And that squeak was his mother's voice saying good night. Mice speak in squeaks, you know."

"Oh," said Baby Bear.

"Now go to sleep," said the big brother bear.

They both snuggled down under the bed covers and shut their eyes to go to sleep. Then deep in the wall they heard a tap and a rap and a snap.

Baby Bear and the big brother bear sat straight up in
their bed.

"What was that?" they called out in the darkness.

Then they both skedaddled out of bed,
down the hall,

and *swoosh!*

…into bed with the biggest brother bear.

"We heard a tap in the wall," the two bears' voices came from deep down under the covers. "And we heard a rap and a snap."

"Why, there's nothing to be frightened of," said the biggest brother bear. "Those noises you heard were little spiders getting ready for bed."

"That tap was a little spider who had finished brushing his teeth and was tapping the water off his toothbrush. That rap was the rap of his hairbrush as he laid it down on the dresser after brushing his hair. And that snap was the light being turned out by his mother when she came to tuck him in and say good night."

"Oh," said the two bears.

"Now let's go to sleep," said the biggest brother bear.

So all three snuggled down under the bed covers and shut their eyes to go to sleep. Then…way down under the floor they heard a bump and a thump and a clump.

The three bears sat straight up in the bed.

"What was that?" they called out in the darkness. Then they all skedaddled out of bed, down the hall, and *swoosh!* into bed with their mama and papa.

"We heard a bump under the floor," the three bears cried from way down under the covers near the mama and papa bears' feet. "And we heard a thump and a clump!"

"Why, there's nothing to be frightened of," said the mama bear. "That bump was a little bug taking off his shoes, getting ready for bed. He let one of the shoes drop with a bump on the hard dirt floor."

"That thump was the little bug thumping up his pillow to make it nice and comfortable. That clump was the little bug's picture book hitting the floor. You see, the little bug's mother had already told him good night five times, but instead of going to sleep, he began looking at his picture book.

"Then he heard his mother coming back to check on him. He threw the book to the floor with a clump and squeezed his eyes shut and hurried and went to sleep. You'll probably hear him snoring any minute."

"Oh," said the three bears, listening very hard because they had never heard a bug snore before.

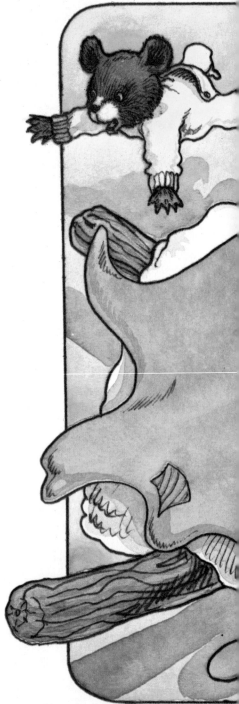

"This bed is too full," said the papa bear. "Skedaddle back to your own beds now, and go to sleep."

Just then there was an eek, creak, squeak and a tap, rap, snap and a bump, thump, clump and a CRASH!

The whole bed came crashing down!

And all the little mice and the little spiders and the
little bugs sat straight up in their beds and called out in fright,
"WHAT WAS THAT?"